To Ben, Liam and Landon: Thank you for giving me the life experiences and the inspiration from which this story came. I would not have this story to tell without you.

A special thank you to my 'editors' and my biggest fans: my family, friends and support system, especially my parents, Anne and Jack Rafferty and my sweet friend, Barbara Graham.

And a big hug to the team at Mascot Books and to Anais, for her beautiful illustrations...for giving life to love.

-Elyse Rafferty Mitchell

For Peter, who has always supported me to pursue my dream.

-Anais

Requests for permission to make copies of any part of the work should be submitted online at info@mascotbooks.com or mailed to Mascot Books, 560 Herndon Parkway #120, Herndon, VA 20170

PRT1111A

Printed in the United States.

ISBN-13: 978-1-936319-87-9
ISBN-10: 1-936319-87-X

www.mascotbooks.com

Meatballs
and
Peanut Butter

Elyse Rafferty Mitchell

Illustrated by
Anais Lee

Liam and Lanny are brothers.

And they are different from each other...

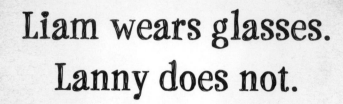

Liam wears glasses.
Lanny does not.

Lanny likes the weather cold.
Liam loves it hot.

Liam is silly and loud.
Lanny is quiet and shy.

The brothers are very different,
but also a lot alike...

Liam loves baseball.
So does Lanny.

Lanny loves the library.
So does Liam.

They both love meatballs.
They both love peanut butter.
And they both know meatballs
and peanut butter don't go together.

Different or the same, they both
love each other very much.
And when it comes to love, they
both agree, Mommy and Daddy
are who they love the best.

But Mommy and Daddy are
different from each other, too.

Mommy loves to run.
Daddy would rather walk.

Daddy loves to sit quietly.
Mommy would rather talk.

Daddy loves sausage on his pizza.
Mommy loves veggies on hers.

Mommy loves to sleep in late.
Daddy's up with the birds.

They both have different jobs.
They both live in different spaces.

Liam and Lanny see them at
different times.
And have toys at both their places.

Different or the same, they both agree, Liam and Lanny are who they love the best.

Shopping:

- milk
- eggs
- toothpaste
- shampoo

It's ok to be the same.
It's ok to be different.
Just like meatballs and peanut
butter, or Mommy and Daddy...

…you can love the same things and you can love the same people. But it doesn't always mean they're good together.

Sometimes people or things go great together.

And sometimes people or things
are better...not together.

...exactly just the same.

About the Author

Elyse Rafferty Mitchell is new to single parenthood, but no stranger to trying to find the right words. With her background in advertising, print, and paper, writing children's books is a perfect, and personally therapeutic, way for her to help her own children better understand the changes happening at home. She lives and works in Chicago with her two boys. She enjoys reading to her children, loves all things creative and cherishes the little moments with her two main guys.

About the Illustrator

Anais Lee is a Taiwanese artist and designer. She has been creating illustrations for books, stationery, and private clients internationally. She lives in Jersey City, New Jersey, with her dog Punchy. Her website is www.anaislee.com.